W9-CFE-559

# Valentine
# Mice!

# Valentine Mice!

by **Bethany Roberts**

Illustrated by **Doug Cushman**

**Green Light Readers**
HOUGHTON MIFFLIN HARCOURT
Boston   New York

First Green Light Readers edition, 2016

All rights reserved. Originally published in hardcover in the United States by
Clarion Books, an imprint of Houghton Mifflin Harcourt Publishing Company,
1997.

Green Light Readers® and its logo are trademarks of HMH publishers LLC,
registered in the United States and other countries.

For information about permission to reproduce selections from this book, write
to trade.permissions@hmhco.com or to Permissions, Houghton Mifflin Harcourt
Publishing Company, 3 Park Avenue, 19th Floor, New York, New York 10016.

www.hmhco.com

The Library of Congress has cataloged the hardcover edition as follows:

Roberts, Bethany.
Valentine mice!/by Bethany Roberts; illustrated by Doug Cushman.
p.  cm.
Summary: An energetic group of mice deliver valentines to the other animals.
[1. Valentines—Fiction. 2. Mice—Fiction.] I. Cushman, Doug, ill. II. Title.
PZ7.R5396Val                                        1997
[E]—dc21                                        96-50889
                                                           CIP
                                                           AC

ISBN: 978-0-395-77518-9 hardcover
ISBN: 978-0-547-37144-3 board book
ISBN: 978-0-544-80898-0 GLR paperback
ISBN: 978-0-544-80897-3 GLR paper over board

Manufactured in China
SCP 10 9 8 7 6 5 4 3 2 1

4500615597

*To my valentines, Bob,*
*Krista and Melissa —B.R.*

*To Juney Irene Cushman,*
*my first valentine*
*—D.C.*

Valentine mice
deliver valentines—

red, pink.
Skip! Hop!

Up this hill,
then s-l-i-d-e down.

One little mouse
goes *swoosh!* Plop!

One to the rabbit,
two for the squirrels,

three for the chipmunks.
Zip! Nip!

More to deliver.

Cross the pond.

S-l-i-d-e!          G-l-i-d-e!

Slip!                    Flip!

Valentines here!

Valentines there!

Shower valentines!

# THROW! THROW! THROW!

Valentine mice—
one, two, three . . .

One is missing!
Where can he be?

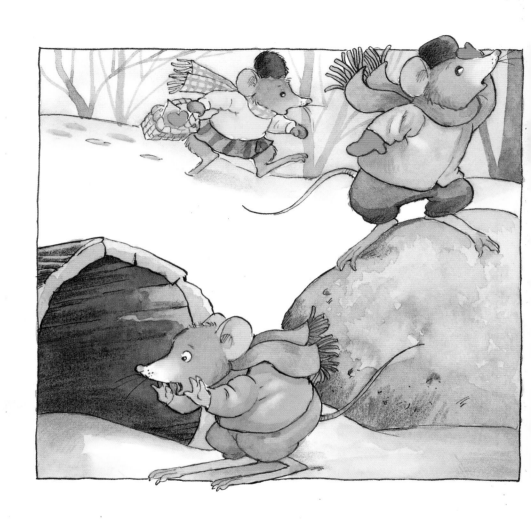

Valentine mice
look high and low.

Hurry! Worry!
Call! Shout!

Follow these footprints.
Quick! Quick!

There's a mitten!

*Pull him out!*

All together now . . .

Dig!                    Tug!

Push!            P-u-l-l!

YAY!

One little mouse gets a

valentine hug.